The
SCAREDY
Cat

Russell Punter

Illustrated by Gustavo Mazali

Reading Consultant: Alison Kelly
Roehampton University

There was once a cat who
lived in a big town.

His name was Stanley.

But everyone called him Scaredy Cat...

...because he was scared of everything.

He was scared of planes...

...and trains.

He was scared of boys...

Help!

...and noise.

He was scared of heights...

...and kites.

He was scared of frogs...

...and dogs.

Stanley was the biggest
scaredy cat in town.

One night, Stanley went for a walk with his friends, Tabby and Snowy.

Something small and furry ran past. A mouse!

"Let's chase it," said Tabby.
"Let's not," cried Stanley.

The mouse ran into
a house.

"It looks like no one is home," said Snowy.

"Here's a cat flap," said Tabby. "Let's go in."

"What if the house is haunted?" said Stanley. He shivered.

But he followed his friends inside.

"Now where's that mouse?" said Tabby.

Suddenly, the mouse ran across the hall and down to the cellar.

"This way!" said Snowy.

Come on!

Snowy and Tabby raced downstairs.

"It's too dark down there," said Stanley. "I'll stay here."

Scaredy Cat!

Now Stanley was all alone, he felt *really* scared.

"M...m...maybe I should have gone with them after all," he thought.

Just then, Stanley felt
a bump. Something was
in the lounge.

"W...w...what was that?"
he wondered.

It went "Bang..."

"Bang!"

"Bang!"

"Come quickly, Snowy!"
called Stanley. "There's a
giant in the lounge."

22

Snowy raced up the stairs.
"A giant?" he cried. "Are
you sure?"

Snowy crept into the
lounge.

"It's just a window
banging," Snowy said.

"Well, it *could* have been a
giant," said Stanley.

"You're such a scaredy cat," said Snowy. "I've got a mouse to catch."

Snowy ran back downstairs.

Just then, Stanley heard
a noise. Something was in
the bathroom.

"W...w...what was that?"
he wondered.

It went "Woo..."

"Wooo!"

"Woooo!"

"Come quickly, Tabby!" called Stanley. "There's a ghost in the bathroom."

28

Tabby raced upstairs.
"A ghost?" he cried. "Are
you sure?"

Tabby crept into the
bathroom.

"It's only the wind,"
Tabby said.

Wooooooooooooo!

"Well, it *might* have been a
ghost," said Stanley.

"You're such a scaredy cat," said Tabby. "I've got a mouse to catch."

Tabby ran back downstairs.

Just then, Stanley saw a lump behind the curtains.

"W...w...what's that?"
he wondered.

It went "Grunt..."

"Grunt!"

"Grunt!"

"Come quickly, Snowy!"
yelled Stanley. "There's a
monster in the lounge."

34

"I don't believe you," called out Snowy.

It's coming to get us!

The monster came closer.

"I don't believe you," called out Tabby.

The monster came closer still.

It came closer... and closer... and closer.

Now it was right on top of Stanley.

Stanley tried to run. But he was frozen to the spot with fear.

The monster tripped
over Stanley.

Wah!

It got tangled in
the curtain...

spun around and
around...

and fell, with a
thud! on the floor.

Snowy and Tabby
came upstairs.

The lady who lived in the
house came home.

Hey, what happened?

A head came through
the curtains.

But it wasn't a monster.

44

The lady stroked Stanley.
"Looks like you just caught
a burglar, kitty-cat."

For the first time in his
life, Stanley felt brave.

The lady gave Stanley
a special reward for
catching the burglar.

You're a hero.

Well done,
Stanley!

From then on, Stanley wasn't afraid of anything.

And no one called him a scaredy cat ever again.

Series editor:
Lesley Sims

First published in 2008 by Usborne Publishing Ltd., Usborne House,
83-85 Saffron Hill, London EC1N 8RT, England. www.usborne.com
Copyright © 2008 Usborne Publishing Ltd.